WITHDRAWN FROM STOCK

KT-385-156

THE NAUGHTIEST UNICORN

AND THE SPOOKY SURPRISE

PIP BIRD

ILLUSTRATED BY DAVID O'CONNELL

EGMONT

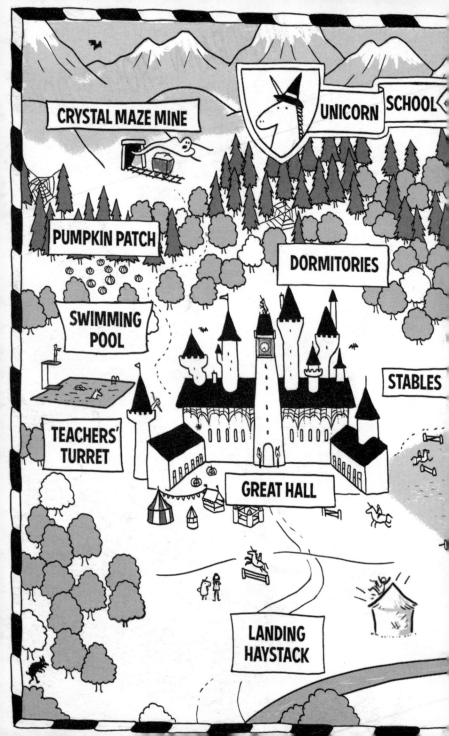

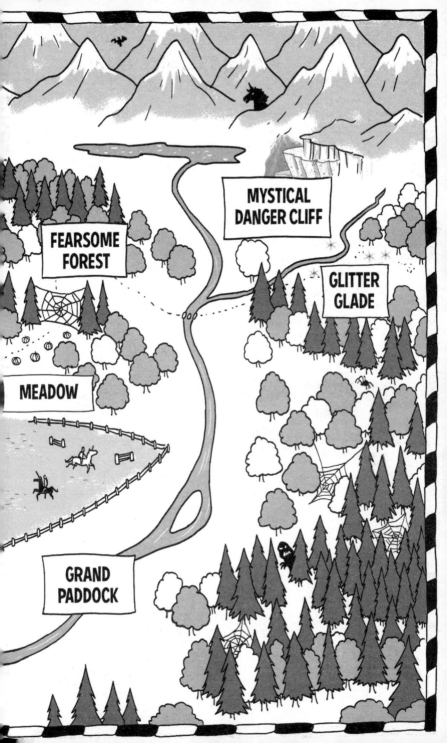

Contents

CHAPTER ONE
Countdown to Halloween

'It was very nearly Halloween and everything was dark and spooky. . .'

The wind rattled the windows of the Unicorn School dormitory.

'. . . everything was dark and spooky AND it was also *super windy*,' continued Mira.

She was holding a torch under her chin to make her face look extra spooky. Everyone in Class Red was there – along with their UBFFs (Unicorn Best Friends Forever).

They were all gathered around Mira, listening as she told her spooky sleepover story. Halloween was just two days away, and everyone was very excited. At Unicorn School, Halloween was celebrated for a whole WEEK, not just one day!

'As the storm raged, a brave girl and her unicorn made their way towards the Scary Forest of Death,' continued Mira.

Thunder rumbled in the distance. Then lightning flashed, lighting up the room.

'Cool!' said Darcy. Darcy was one of Mira's best friends at Unicorn School.

Raheem's unicorn, Brave, gave a high-pitched squeal and hid his head under a pillow.

2

'Why would they go to the Forest of Death?' said Jake.

'Um,' said Mira, thinking quickly. 'There was something they really needed to get from the shops, and the only way to get there was through the Forest of Death.'

'That makes sense,' said Raheem thoughtfully. Raheem was Mira's other best friend.

'So, the girl and her unicorn had just got to the forest,' said Mira, 'and they heard a rustling in the bushes.'

Everyone jumped as a strange rustling sound came from behind Mira. She looked around in surprise. Her unicorn, Dave, was opening a large packet of sour sweets shaped like mini ghouls.

Mira grinned and gave her UBFF a scratch behind the ears.

Dave wasn't like the other unicorns at Unicorn School. They were mostly glittery, magical and pranced elegantly around, being very well-behaved. Dave was grumpy, greedy and interrupted most lessons by doing giant poos

or falling asleep and snoring loudly.

'Get on with the story, I want to tell mine!' said Jake.

Mira frowned at Jake. 'So . . . they heard a rustling in the bushes, and then . . . a big witch jumped out.'

'How big was she?' asked Tamsin.

Mira thought. 'Bigger than a car, but smaller than a dinosaur.'

'Did she have a black caticorn?' said Seb.

'Did she have a SLOTH?' said Flo. Flo loved sloths and slothicorns.

'Both!' said Mira.

'Yay!' shouted Flo and Seb.

'The big witch, her black caticorn and her sloth

CHASED the girl and the unicorn,' said Mira.

Flo and Seb gasped. Their unicorns, Sparkles and Firework, shivered and whinnied excitedly.

'The girl and the unicorn managed to do a spell and turn the witch into a tiny toad, but now it was completely dark and they were lost,' said Mira. 'All around them it was silent. Suddenly –'

PAARRRRRRRPPP!

Dave's giant fart rocketed around the room like a thunderclap.

All the children screamed loudly. The unicorns shrieked and Brave bolted and hid in a cupboard.

'Oh, Dave!' said Mira, grinning at her unicorn. She loved it when Dave joined in with her stories, even if it was by accident. Even though Dave wasn't *quite* the sparkly, glittering Unicorn Best Friend Forever Mira had dreamed of before she'd started Unicorn School, she still thought he was the best unicorn in the whole WORLD.

Mira went to give him a hug. Dave took the opportunity to stick his nose straight into her plastic pumpkin snack bucket and started chomping on the snacks that were in there.

'My turn to tell a story!' said Jake. He grabbed the torch from Mira and held it under his chin. 'My story is called the Terrifying Tale of the Spookicorn.'

'Ooooooh,' said Class Red, snuggling into their sleeping bags.

'I've heard of the Spookicorn!' said Tamsin.

'I didn't know it had a terrifying tail, though,' said Flo.

Jake's unicorn, Pegasus, shushed them.

'It was a dark and spooky night . . .' said Jake.

'I've heard that the Spookicorn is the spookiest of all unicorns,' said Seb. His unicorn Firework nodded wisely.

'And it has red eyes,' said Flo.

'When it arrives somewhere it knocks three times and then does a bone-chilling neigh,' said Darcy.

'Sshhh!' said Jake. 'You're spoiling the story!

As I was SAYING,' he continued, 'it was a dark and spooky night. AND it was a full moon. A really cool boy and his unicorn were all alone. Do you know where they were?'

'In a creepy old castle?' said Seb.

'In space?' said Flo.

'In the zombie apocalypse?' said Darcy.

'No,' said Jake. 'They were here, at Unicorn School.'

A hush descended on the dorm. Mira felt a little shiver go up her spine.

'It was nearly midnight, and the really cool boy and his unicorn were having a midnight feast. And then, there was a knock at the door.'

KNOCK KNOCK KNOCK

The unicorns all jumped in fright. Jake shone the torch around the room.

The light fell on Dave. His face was stuck in the plastic pumpkin treat bucket, and he was banging it on the floor to try and get it off.

Mira grabbed the bucket with both hands and tugged. Raheem and Freya joined her. Eventually they managed to pull the bucket off Dave's head.

Jake narrowed his eyes at Dave. 'ANYWAY, it was Halloween, it was a full moon and it was midnight. And it was really spooky. And there was a knock at the door. And –'

KNOCK KNOCK KNOCK

'Dave, stop it!' said Jake.

But Dave was now snoring quietly on top of a mountain of sweet wrappers.

Lightning flashed in the windows. A rumble of thunder followed quickly.

Mira shivered. If Dave hadn't made the knocking noise . . . who – or what – had?

CHAPTER TWO
A Mysterious Stranger . . .

'I think it was someone knocking at the front door,' said Mira.

'Maybe it's the Spookicorn. Let's investigate!' yelled Darcy.

'Let's NOT,' said Jake.

'I want to see the Spookicorn!' said Flo, standing up beside Darcy.

'Me too,' said Mira. 'Come on, Jake – it will be just like in your story.'

'Okay, fine!' said Jake. 'But I'm not going first.'

Mira nudged Dave, who farted himself awake. Then she and her friends and their UBFFs all crept out of the dorm. They tiptoed and tiphoofed along the corridor to the staircase into the hallway. The rain drummed on the roof and the moonlight shone through the high windows, casting strange shadows all around.

'So spooky!' whispered Mira to Dave.

'BURP,' Dave agreed.

'Look!' whispered Darcy.

Madame Shetland, the Unicorn School headteacher, was standing by the large front door.

The door opened with a long creak.

There was another flash of lightning. Mira gulped. Outside in the gloom, there loomed a figure in a wide-brimmed hat and cloak.

'Do come in out of the storm,' Madame Shetland said.

Thunder boomed outside.

The clock struck midnight.

The cloaked figure stepped inside.

The children and their unicorns turned and sprinted back towards the dorm. Who was the mysterious figure that had arrived in the dead of night . . . ?

'Happy Halloween!' Madame Shetland, the Unicorn School headteacher, greeted the pupils as they walked into assembly the next morning.

Mira was excited to see that the Grand Hall had been decorated for Halloween. The entire hall ceiling was covered in sparkly cobwebs, the rows of chairs were draped in black and orange glittery streamers and there were inflatable unicorn skeletons dotted around the indoor paddock.

Class Red had spent the whole morning talking about the mysterious stranger who'd arrived in the storm. Who could it be? Tamsin thought it was a big witch. Darcy thought it was a Zombie Ghost Princess. Flo thought it was

either a new teacher or a yeti.

Mira took her notebook out of her bag.
The notebook was new, and would be perfect
for taking notes about mysteries. (She knew
this was what all great detectives do.) She wrote
down:

Mysterious stranger
Big witch?
Zombie ghost princess??

On the stage behind Madame Shetland, the
teachers sat down in their seats. Mira couldn't

see anyone new. But then she realised one of the seats was empty. Where was Miss Glitterhorn?

Madame Shetland clapped her hands to shush the pupils and their unicorns.

'Now, as many of you may know,' said the headteacher, 'unicorns love all things spooky, which is why at Unicorn School we celebrate Halloween all week long!'

Mira felt an excited tingling in her tummy. Her sister Rani had been going to Unicorn School for two years and had told her about all the spooky-themed lessons. Mira couldn't wait! She squeezed Dave tightly. Her UBFF gave her a friendly burp.

Madame Shetland continued. 'In two days,

on official Halloween night, we have our
traditional Spooky Fancy Dress Party. But I am
also thrilled to announce that we also have a
special quest . . .'

An 'Ooooooooooh!' travelled around the room.

'What do you think it is, Dave?' whispered Mira.

Dave gave Mira a mysterious look, and then

he did a spooky poo (which was really just a poo). Mira sighed and got out her trusty poo shovel.

'The special quest is the Spooky Surprise Challenge,' said Madame Shetland. 'Whoever creates the spookiest surprise in time for the Halloween Party wins a very special spooky quest medal.'

'Is it a GHOST medal?' said Darcy.

'Hand up to ask a question please, Darcy,' said Madame Shetland.

'Is it a GHOST medal?' said Darcy, putting her hand up.

'What's a ghost medal?' said Jake.

'It's a medal that died hundreds of years ago and haunts the corridors looking for revenge,' said Darcy.

'Can I just have a normal medal, not a ghost one?' said Tamsin, putting her hand up.

'Hold on. Nobody has won the quest yet!' said Madame Shetland sternly. 'You may create your spooky surprise alone, in pairs, or as a whole class, but every single pupil and their unicorn must enter the challenge!'

All the pupils were chatting noisily about their spooky surprise ideas, so Madame Shetland

22

called an end to assembly and told everyone to go to their classrooms to start lessons.

'Make sure you all start thinking about your spooky surprise,' she called after them. 'And Class Red?'

Mira and the others stopped and looked back.

'Miss Glitterhorn is . . . away this week,' said Madame Shetland. 'So you have a supply teacher – he's waiting for you in the classroom.'

ꙮ ꙮ ꙮ

Mira threw Dave some pumpkin sweets to catch as they walked down the corridor to their classroom.

'What do you think has happened to Miss Glitterhorn?' said Raheem.

'I heard she was poisoned by the school dinners,' said Tamsin.

Dave snorted as if to say no way. Dave loved Unicorn School dinners.

'Actually, she was abducted by aliens,' said Darcy.

'Are you sure? I haven't read about any aliens at Unicorn School,' said Raheem. He was thumbing through a book called *The Dangers of Halloween at Unicorn School*.

'Of course there aren't any aliens here,' said Darcy.

Raheem breathed a sigh of relief.

'ANY MORE,' Darcy added. 'Because they've abducted Miss Glitterhorn and taken

her back to their home planet.'

'I'd love to go on holiday with an alien,' said Flo.

'I think Miss Glitterhorn was actually a zombie in disguise and they caught her trying to eat everyone's brains,' said Darcy.

Star snorted in agreement and Darcy gave her UBFF a hoof-five.

Mira nodded and chewed her pen. It certainly looked like there was a mystery! She wrote '*Miss Glitterhorn – zombie in disguise?*' in her notebook.

'Er, guys,' interrupted Freya.

They'd reached the classroom, but the door was shut and all the lights were off.

'Maybe the teacher's not here yet?' said Mira.

There was a pause while they all looked
at each other. No one wanted to go in first.
Everyone nudged each other until Mira was
at the front of the group. Tamsin grabbed
Mira's hand, knocked on the door with her

knuckles, and ran back behind everyone else.

With a **CRREEEAAAAAK** the door

opened. A shadowy figure in a hat and cloak

stood in the doorway.

'Welcome, Class Red,' said a deep voice.

'I've been DYING to meet you!'

CHAPTER THREE
Weird Science

Class Red reluctantly entered their classroom and sat down. All the curtains were closed and the lights were switched off. It was very hard to see. Dave tripped over a desk and bumped into Jake, sending him sprawling across the tables.

'Oh! Sorry,' said the teacher, and turned on the lights.

Now that Mira could see their new teacher, she realised that he was very tall, dressed all in black and had a big bushy beard.

'I was preparing something for your first

lesson,' said the new teacher. 'All will be
revealed soon! My name is Mr Spooky.'

Class Red all looked at each other. Freya's
unicorn, Princess, snorted nervously.

Mr Spooky smiled. 'First, I want
to learn all your names. Then
we've got a super spooky
science lesson to cover.'

★ Weird Science ★

Each human-unicorn pair stood up and introduced themselves. Mr Spooky was smiling away. Mira thought he looked like the friendliest teacher they'd ever had. Miss Glitterhorn was very friendly too, but she did sometimes get cross when Dave interrupted her lessons with farts.

'Now it's time to start the spooky science lesson,' said Mr Spooky. 'We're going to

be making SLIME. Come and collect your ingredients and instruction sheets!'

'YAAAAAY!' yelled Class Red, leaping up from their desks.

'Do you think it's a bit strange that Mr Spooky showed up just when Miss Glitterhorn disappeared?' whispered Tamsin a few minutes later as she stirred her slime.

'There's definitely something spooky about him,' Raheem whispered back.

'He's the Zombie Ghost Princess,' whispered Darcy.

'I think he's great,' said Flo, carefully writing 'FLO' in slime on her bag. Flo's unicorn Sparkles dipped her horn in the

slime bucket. Dave tried to eat some but spat it out in disgust.

'Come on guys,' whispered Jake. 'It's obvious what's going on.'

They all looked at him.

'Mr Spooky is a *vampire*,' said Jake.

'How do you know?' said Darcy.

'I just know this stuff,' said Jake, crossing his arms. 'Why do you think he's got the blinds down? It's because vampires shrivel up in sunlight. AND you've all missed the OTHER most important thing.'

'What's that?' asked Tamsin shakily.

Jake pointed at the teacher. 'He has very, very sharp teeth,' he said.

'Hmm,' said Darcy. 'I'm still thinking Zombie Ghost Princess.'

'Actually, I think Jake could be right,' said Raheem. He pointed to a page in his *Dangers of Halloween* book.

Fun vampire facts!

Vampires . . .

- shrivel up in sunlight
- don't appear in mirrors or photos
- have very, very sharp teeth
- are allergic to garlic
- drink blood

Mira gasped. She wrote *'Mr Spooky – vampire??'* in her notebook.

'Well, even if Mr Spooky is a vampire, and he ate Miss Glitterhorn with his very, very sharp teeth, how do we prove it?' said Darcy.

'Mr Spooky,' said Raheem, putting his hand up. 'I prefer to make slime in natural light. Could we open the blinds?'

'NO!' shouted Mr Spooky. There was a pause and then he laughed. 'It will spoil the fun – you'll see!'

The children and their unicorns all looked at each other. Then they looked back at Raheem's book. Dave poked his horn at the sentence that read *shrivel up in sunlight*.

'Does anyone have a mirror?' whispered Jake.

'I've got my phone,' said Darcy. She opened the camera, pointed the phone at Mr Spooky and clicked. She checked the screen. 'There's nobody there!' she said.

Mira held her breath. Was Mr Spooky *really* a vampire? She looked up at the front of the classroom where Mr Spooky was sitting at the desk. And then she froze.

There was something red and sticky on Mr Spooky's beard!

Mira, Darcy, Jake, Raheem and their unicorns all gasped.

And then all the lights went out.

'Arghhhh!' shrieked Class Red and the unicorns screamed. Mira shut her eyes. Some people dived under the desks. Dave jumped into Mira's arms. And then . . .

'That's AWESOME!' said Flo.

Mira opened her eyes. It was pitch black,

but she could see the name FLO glowing in the
dark. What was going on? Then she realised.
All the pots of slime were glowing in the dark!
They twinkled different rainbow colours.
Next to Flo, Sparkles' horn was glowing green.

'Oooooooohhh!' said all the children, climbing
out from under the desks. The unicorns clapped
their hooves.

'Isn't it cool?' came Mr Spooky's voice.
'Glow-in-the-dark slime. It doesn't last for
very long, so look while you can!'

Soon the pots of slime started to fade.
So did Flo's name and Sparkles' horn.

Mr Spooky turned the lights back on.
He reached into a lunchbox and picked out

a half-eaten sandwich. 'I hope you don't mind me having a bite to eat,' he said. 'I skipped breakfast and I couldn't resist a mid-morning snack!' He took a bite of the sandwich. 'Jam sandwiches are my favourite,' he said, wiping a blob of red jam from the corner of his mouth.

Phew, thought Mira. The red stuff around
Mr Spooky's mouth was just jam!

There was a loud NEIGH, the thundering
of hooves and a blur of white next to Mira.
Dave was galloping across the classroom,
heading straight for the jam sandwiches.
But as he went, one of his hooves got tangled
in the cord that pulled the blinds. Dave tripped
and somersaulted forwards – the blind
cord pulled tight, and then . . .

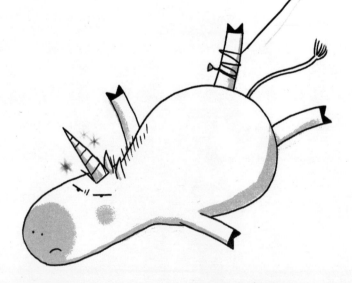

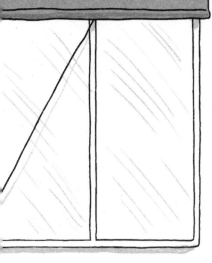

SNAP!

The blinds on all the windows rolled upwards, and soft sunlight flooded into the classroom.

'Ooh the sun's come out. Lovely!' said Mr Spooky, blinking in the bright light.

Darcy peered at Mr Spooky. 'He doesn't look like he's shrivelled up,' she said.

Jake frowned. 'What about the photo you took of him?'

Darcy looked back at her phone. 'Oh sorry, I had the camera the wrong way round. I took a photo of the wall behind me instead.'

CHAPTER FOUR
Spooky Mr Spooky

'So I guess Mr Spooky isn't a vampire and probably didn't eat Miss Glitterhorn with his very, very sharp teeth,' said Raheem, as Class Red and their unicorns sat in the dining hall

eating their Halloween-themed lunch. Dave had already eaten his and was trying to steal everyone else's food.

'Hmm,' said Jake grumpily as he put his fork through his worm spaghetti (which was actually just normal spaghetti).

'I think it's cool they've called all the food spooky names,' said Mira.

MENU
WORM SPAGHETTI
BOGEYS
EYEBALLS
BLOODY VICTORIA
SPONGE AND SNOT

'They do it every year.'

The voice came from the table next to them, where Mira's big sister Rani was sitting with her friends. Rani popped an eyeball (a grape) into her mouth. 'How's your spooky surprise going?' she said. 'Ours is going to be totally awesome.'

Mira looked at Darcy and Raheem in panic. They hadn't even thought of an idea yet! 'Um . . .' she said.

Luckily Rani got distracted by Dave snaffling a grape eyeball from her bowl. Rani swatted him away.

'What spooky lessons have you been doing?' said Mira, changing the subject. She would

make sure they thought of a really good spooky surprise idea and start working on it that afternoon!

'We were doing Spooky Maths with Class Green,' said Rani's friend, Lois. 'It was just like normal maths really but Ms Fetlock was dressed as a witch.'

'That sounds cool,' said Mira.

'How come you were with Class Green?' said Darcy as she swallowed a mouthful of bogeys (spinach).

'Mr Nosebag is away,' said a boy next to Lois. 'We saw him at registration, but then Madame Shetland came and said he'd had to go. Isn't your teacher away too?'

'Yeah,' replied Darcy. 'We've got Mr Spooky as a substitute teacher. No one's told us why Miss Glitterhorn is missing. We think he ate her.'

'Well, we don't think that any more,' said Freya.

'It is a *bit* strange that both our teachers have gone,' said Mira.

'Losing one teacher is unlucky, but losing two just seems careless,' said Flo, as she plaited Sparkles' hair with worm spaghetti.

'And it was just when Mr Spooky arrived,' said Raheem thoughtfully. Next to him, Brave and Star were flicking through the *Dangers of Halloween* book. 'There's definitely something spooky about Mr Spooky, apart from his name, but we can't work out what.'

'Well, good luck with that,' said Rani. 'We'd love to help, but we've got an awesome spooky surprise to do! I hope you find out what type of monster he is before he eats all the teachers and you.'

'Thanks!' said Flo, waving as Rani and her friends picked up their trays and left.

'So,' said Darcy. 'If Mr Spooky isn't a vampire, then what is he? A Zombie Ghost Princess?'

Mira and her friends all had a think. Dave finished off everyone's Bloody Victoria Sponge and Snot (Victoria jam sponge and custard).

Then Mira heard voices outside the window. She turned to see Mr Spooky walking with Madame Shetland. She signalled to the others,

and they all held their breath and tried to hear what the teachers were saying.

'Class Red are just brilliant,' said Mr Spooky.

'I'm glad it's going well, Mr Spooky,' said Madame Shetland outside the window. 'Shall I see you at the special Full Moon staff meeting tonight?'

'I don't think I can,' said Mr Spooky. 'There's something important I have to do . . .'

The two teachers walked further away from the window, and Mira couldn't hear what they were saying any more. What was the important thing that Mr Spooky had to do?

There was a sudden snort from Star. She and Brave were still looking through Raheem's book together. Star pointed her hoof at the open page, and Brave gave a whinny.

Wonderful things about WEREWOLVES!

Werewolves . . .
- *are very hairy*
- *transform on a full moon*
- *have a terrifying howl*

Mira looked at her friends. Mr Spooky did have a very big beard. Could he really be a WEREWOLF? She updated her notebook.

After lunch, Class Red had music with Ms Dazzleflank. Mira and her friends headed to the music rooms.

'We have to make our spooky surprise idea really good,' said Mira. 'I'm going to start a list.' She definitely wouldn't let herself get distracted by vampires again. Or werewolves. Or Zombie Ghost Princesses. She took out her notebook and wrote a new title.

Really Good Spooky Surprise Ideas

They had reached the classroom door, and they could hear a strange noise coming from the other side.

'AAAAWWOOOOOOO!'

'That sounds werewolfy!' said Mira, putting her notebook back in her bag.

Brave turned straight around on his hooves and cantered away. Raheem went to get him. Darcy wheeled forwards and pushed the classroom door. It opened to reveal . . .

'Mr Spooky!' said Flo.

CHAPTER FIVE
Bat Raps and Phantom Football

'Hello again, Class Red!' said the teacher, stroking his big bushy beard and smiling widely, showing his long shiny teeth. 'I was just having a little sing-song. Now, I'm afraid poor Ms Dazzleflank is, uh, unavailable, so I'm taking your music class today. Come on in.'

'Another teacher not here? Hmm, suspicious,' stage-whispered Darcy as she rolled through the doors.

The chairs were all set up in a circle around

the grand piano, next to a microphone stand.

'I see from Ms Dazzleflank's notes that you were learning the history of unicorn karaoke,' said Mr Spooky, as Class Red all sat down. 'I don't know much about that, but I thought today we would have a practical lesson. And – oh!'

Darcy was already at the microphone, ready to perform.

'Hit it!' said Darcy, as Star sat down behind the grand piano.

Everyone clapped along as Darcy performed a spooky song called the Bat Rap. Mira joined in the singing as loudly as everybody else, but Dave had taken her tambourine to use as a

pillow. He always liked to have a nap in the music room.

'Now my next song,' said Darcy, 'is called "Mr Spooky is a Were—'

Mr Spooky banged his tambourine. 'That was wonderful, Darcy!' he said. 'But I think it's time for someone else to have a go.'

Flo grabbed the microphone and performed 'Zombie Opera'.

Next, Seb, Tamsin and Freya, who were in a band together, got up and played a song called 'Monster Unicorn Rock'. Class Red went wild.

Then Mr Spooky said he was going to sing them a bit of his favourite type of music, which was called 'heavy metal'.

'**AAAAWWOOOOOOO!**' he howled.

'My ears!' squealed Tamsin. Her unicorn, Moondance, put her head in Tamsin's schoolbag.

'That is one terrifying howl,' whispered Raheem, pointing at the page of the *Dangers of Halloween* book.

'And he's very hairy,' said Darcy. 'Look at that beard.'

Mira nodded. It was all starting to make sense. 'It's a full moon tonight,' she said. 'So if he is a werewolf, that's when he'll properly transform. And we know he's going to be in the Pumpkin Patch!'

'Maybe we can sneak out and catch him!' whispered Darcy.

'AWWWOOOOOOOOOOOOOO YEAH'

screamed Mr Spooky, throwing his arms into the air. He took a bow. 'Does anyone else want a go, or shall I do another one?'

All the hands and hooves in the room went up in the air. So for the rest of the lesson they all took turns to perform, finishing up with a fifteen-minute fart solo from Dave.

'Wonderful,' said Mr Spooky as they started to file out of the music room. 'So many new tunes for me to sing on my full-moon evening walk.'

∪∪∪

On the way to their PE lesson, Class Red walked past some kids from Class Blue who were working on a huge painting that they wouldn't let anyone look at. They also passed a

girl from Class Green who had a bucket of apples

that she was drawing faces on.

'I don't know if Mr Spooky IS a werewolf,' said Jake. 'It seems a bit far-fetched.'

'But he's really hairy, like a werewolf,' said Darcy. 'We all heard him howl, *like a werewolf*. AND he's going for a full-moon evening walk. LIKE A WEREWOLF.' Star neighed in agreement.

Jake sighed. 'Fine, he's a werewolf,' he said.

'You know what we have to do,' said Darcy.

'Tell Madame Shetland and then stay a safe distance away until he's caught?' said Raheem.

'No,' said Darcy. 'We have to go out tonight, catch Mr Spooky turning into a werewolf, and basically save EVERYONE's life! Well,

apart from the teachers he has already eaten.
It's too late for them.'

Mira took out her notebook again and wrote
a new title. She realised that they *still* hadn't had
any great ideas for their spooky surprise. It was
very time consuming, trying to work out who –
or WHAT – Mr Spooky was!

'I should be team leader,' said Jake.

'*I'm* leader because the plan is my idea,' said
Darcy, and everyone agreed that this was fair.

'Okay, but I get to be Monster Expert,'
said Jake.

'Raheem is Monster Expert, but you can be
his assistant,' said Darcy.

They were almost at the football pitch now.

The unicorns started to organise themselves
into teams.

PHWWEEEET!

Hearing the whistle, Mira looked around for
the PE teacher, Miss Hind. Miss Hind always
got a bit cross if the football matches didn't kick
off on time.

But it wasn't Miss Hind.

It was . . .

'Hey gang!' said Mr Spooky. He was wearing
a rainbow tracksuit and doing stretches at the
side of the pitch. 'I'm afraid Miss Hind can't be
here for a mysterious unknown reason. So I'll
be taking your PE lesson!'

Mr Spooky explained that they would be

playing ghost football, which was just like normal football, except the ball was invisible.

'How will we know what the score is?' said Darcy.

'You won't,' said Mr Spooky. 'That's why it's so super fun. Everyone's a winner!'

So they all played ghost football. It was quite confusing, and very hard to tell where the ball was, and Darcy said it was 'the worst game I've ever played'. But at least while the rest of the class were arguing about whether or not Sparkles had done a hoofball, Mira and her friends could discuss their plan to catch Mr Spooky turning into a werewolf.

Mira wrote down in her notebook:

CATCH A WEREWOLF PLAN!

1. Find out when Mr Spooky's evening walk is and where he is going.

Mr Spooky was refereeing the game, but also still doing his stretches. 'Just getting ready for my walk!' he said.

Mira looked at her friends. Dave burped meaningfully.

'What time do you go on your walk?' said Mira, taking an imaginary throw-in.

'Seven o'clock on the dot,' said Mr Spooky. 'Can't miss dinner!'

Dave gave a loud fart of approval.

'Plus I know the Pumpkin Patch will look lovely in the full moon,' said Mr Spooky.

'That was easy!' said Mira to herself, writing down *7pm – Pumpkin Patch*.

Next they had to work out how they would get out of school to follow Mr Spooky. Darcy said they should sneak out, but Raheem thought they should get permission. Mira wrote in her notebook, *2. Sneak out of school (with permission)*.

In the match, Princess was celebrating a hat trick, but Tamsin pointed out she was so far offside she wasn't even on the pitch any more. Meanwhile, Mira, Jake, Darcy and Raheem couldn't agree on the best way to lay a werewolf trap. But, after a LOT of discussion, the Catch a Werewolf plan was ready!

Mira clutched her notebook to her chest.

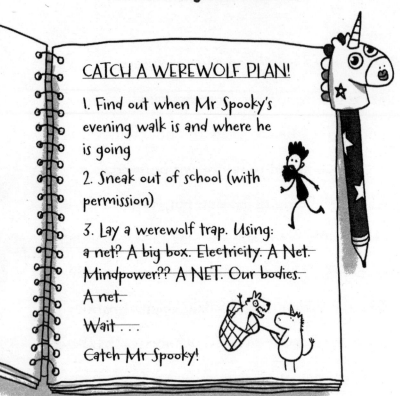

CATCH A WEREWOLF PLAN!

1. Find out when Mr Spooky's evening walk is and where he is going

2. Sneak out of school (with permission)

3. Lay a werewolf trap. Using: a net? A big box. Electricity. A Net. Mindpower?? A NET. Our bodies. A net.

Wait . . .

Catch Mr Spooky!

This was turning out to be the spookiest Halloween EVER! If their plan worked and they managed to catch Mr Spooky, they would save the school! Mira did a little excited dance, just as a cheer went up from the football field.

Dave had done a big, round, football-shaped

poo.

Mira looked around for her poo shovel.

She'd left it in the PE changing rooms!

But then there was another cheer as Dave

trotted forward and kicked the poo to Brave.

Brave dribbled the poo-ball around Sparkles

and passed it to Freya. It was much easier playing

with a ball of poo than the invisible ball.

'Here, here!' called Mira, running down

the wing.

'Great stuff, Class Red!' called Mr Spooky.

Mira crossed the poo into the box, and Darcy

headed it into the goal. Then Dave did three

more football-poos and everyone started kicking

them into the goals. They all agreed that ghost

football was fun, but poo-ball was the best

game ever!

CHAPTER SIX
Time to Catch a Werewolf

A few hours later, Mira and Dave were making their way to the stables. They were going to meet the others in Pegasus's stable, and then make their way to the Fearsome Forest to catch Mr Spooky turning into a werewolf.

'Are you excited, Dave?' Mira gave her unicorn a scratch behind the ears.

Dave nodded his little head and gave an excited burp. So Mira fed him the first of his mission snacks, and he burped even louder.

They reached the door of Pegasus's stable and knocked. The stable door opened a tiny bit and Jake's face appeared, with Pegasus's face just above it.

'What's the secret code word?' he whispered.

'Weasel bum,' Mira whispered back.

'I can't hear you,' whispered Jake.

'WEASEL BUM,' shouted Mira.

'What are you doing?' said her sister Rani from behind her.

Jake quickly shut the stable door.

'Just . . . singing a song,' said Mira. **'WEASEL BUM, WEASEL BUM, la la la WEASEL BUM!'** she sang.

'You're SO weird,' said Rani, as she and her unicorn Angelica walked off.

'Let me in!' hissed Mira through the door.

Jake opened the door. Darcy, Star, Raheem and Brave were there already, sitting on the straw.

'Keep Pegasus's stable tidy and don't touch any of our cool toys,' said Jake. Then he pointed at Dave. 'And don't do any giant poos.'

Dave blinked at Jake. And then he did a giant poo that landed with a THUD on the straw.

Pegasus whinnied in outrage.

Mira opened her rucksack and got out a poo bag (there wasn't space in her bag for the poo shovel). She left the poo in the bag by the door to put in the bins later. Right now they had to start the mission!

'Now, has everyone brought their special monster-fighting kit like I said?' said Jake, bossily.

'I brought the Dangers of Halloween book,'

said Raheem, holding up his rucksack.

'Great,' said Jake. 'What else?'

'Six other books,' said Raheem.

'I brought a few different outfits for Star and me,' said Darcy.

'My whole bag is full of Dave's snacks,' said Mira.

Jake folded his arms. 'How are ANY of those things going to help us catch a werewolf?'

'What have *you* brought then?' said Darcy.

Jake opened his bag, which was covered in a camouflage pattern. Inside was a torch, a pair of night-vision goggles, a large foam blaster gun, walkie talkies, the net to lay the werewolf trap and some energy balls.

'Can I have the gun?' said Darcy.

'No!' said Jake, grabbing everything out of the bag and hugging it all to him.

'Can I wear the goggles?' said Raheem.

Jake quickly put the night-vision goggles on and ran over to the other side of the stable.

Because it was dark with the goggles on, he ran straight into a wall, dropping everything. Dave tiptoed over and ate the energy balls.

Jake stood up, a bit dazed, and then put all the bits of the monster-fighting kit back in his bag. 'We'll just get stuff out when we need it,' he said, mainly to Darcy, who was still eyeing the gun and its supply of foam blasters.

They all went over the plan a few more times, except Dave, who had decided to take a nap on Pegasus's special beanbag. Pegasus snorted crossly and nudged Dave off with his hoof, but Dave just sleep-crawled back again.

Mira suddenly looked up. 'What's the time?' she said.

'My cool watch says it's five to seven!' said Jake, leaping to his feet.

'Mr Spooky will be going on his walk soon!' said Raheem.

'Go! Go! Go!' said Darcy, grabbing her bag of outfits and wheeling to the front of the stable.

The rest of them quickly grabbed their bags and followed her. Mira tipped the beanbag up and Dave rolled on to the straw with a yawn.

It was time to catch a werewolf!

⊍⊍⊍

Wisps of cloud crossed the bright, full moon against an ink-blue sky. Far below, on the frosty grass, four children and their unicorns

crept out from the Unicorn School stables. They darted across the playing fields to the entrance of the Fearsome Forest, one pair at a time.

Mira shivered even though she and Dave were wrapped up in hats, scarves and gloves. When it was their turn, she held a ghost-shaped doughnut on a string to get Dave to trot quickly towards the forest. Then she threw the doughnut behind the bush where everyone was hiding. Dave dived into the bush and gobbled up the doughnut.

Raheem checked the Forbidden Forest map, then pointed the way to the Pumpkin Patch. Everyone nodded and followed as quietly as possible, trying not to crunch the fallen autumn leaves on their way – except Dave, who rolled in the crunchy leaves like a dog.

Soon, Mira could see a small clearing in the trees up ahead. The moon shone through the branches and lit up the forest with a misty glow. Orange pumpkin shapes rose up through the frosty ground.

'Quick, hide!' said Jake.

Jake opened his bag and looked inside. His eyes went wide with horror.

Darcy looked inside Jake's bag. 'Why did you

bring a bag of poo?' she said.

'You must have picked up my poo-bag!' said
Mira.

'I still don't get why he'd bring that instead
of the monster-fighting kit,' said Darcy.

'I didn't do it on PURPOSE,' said Jake. 'It
was dark and we left in a hurry!'

'Don't worry,' said Raheem. 'I have a spare
torch in my emergency bumbag. And I'm sure
we can still make the werewolf trap. We don't
need fancy stuff.'

'Jake's bag had the net in it,' said Darcy. 'Do
you have a spare net?'

'I have a spare pair of socks and a copy of the
school rules,' said Raheem.

They all went silent as everyone tried to think.

Mira looked through her bag, wondering if it was possible to make a net out of snacks.

'Jam sandwiches?' she said, just as Darcy said, 'Let's make the net out of our own hair.'

'What did you say?' said Jake.

'Hair,' said Darcy.

'Jam sandwiches,' said Mira.

'Neither of those things are helpful!' snapped Jake. 'Help me weave these twigs together to make a cage.'

Jake tried to weave two tiny twigs together. They broke. He got up and started moving around the clearing, looking for more twigs.

'Don't do that, Jake,' said Raheem.

'Well, no one has any better ideas!' said Jake, walking around some more.

'I mean, DON'T WALK THERE!' said Raheem.

Jake froze, about to step on to a big pile of leaves.

'Brave and I made a trap while you guys were squabbling,' said Raheem. 'It's a hole with branches and leaves covering it.'

'Nice one, Raheem!' said Mira, grinning at her friend.

They placed a few of the jam sandwiches from Mira's snack rucksack carefully on top of the branches and leaves. Then they hid in the bushes, waiting for Mr Spooky to arrive.

Mira held her breath. Over to the left she could see the Pumpkin Patch, with its orange orbs gleaming in the mist. They were the biggest pumpkins she'd ever seen.

There was a crunching sound along the path. Footsteps!

A shadowy figure was approaching. They all froze, except for Dave, who leaped into Mira's arms.

Next there was an almighty CRASH as the shadowy figure fell into the hole.

The friends cheered.

They'd done it! They'd caught Mr Spooky the werewolf!

CHAPTER SEVEN
The Teacher Trap

They crept over to the edge of Raheem's trap.

Everyone shuffled around to look through a hole

in the branches and saw . . .

'Miss Hind?!' said Jake.

'Who's there?' shouted the PE teacher from

inside the hole. 'Help me out!'

'Errr,' said Mira. The others were slowly

backing away from the trap. Dave had run off

into the Pumpkin Patch. Judging from the

noises, he was tucking into a pumpkin.

Before they could do anything to help

Miss Hind, more crunching footsteps came echoing through the forest. Another shadowy figure was walking through the mist along the path. Mira and her friends jumped back into the bushes. Over in the Pumpkin Patch, Dave carried on eating a particularly juicy pumpkin.

'AWOOOOOOOOOOOOOOOOOOOO!'

As the second shadowy figure got closer, they could hear the howling. This time, it was definitely Mr Spooky.

'Awoooooooooo! Yeah!' sang Mr Spooky. 'Ooh, what's this? Jam sandwiches! Don't mind if I d—'

'Is that you, Mr Spooky?' called Miss Hind from inside the trap.

Mira peered through the bushes as Mr Spooky helped Miss Hind out of the hole. The full moon shone down on him through the trees. He definitely hadn't transformed into a werewolf.

'I was so sure we were right,' whispered Raheem.

'I *knew* he wasn't a werewolf,' said Jake.

'Zombie Ghost Princess . . .' whispered

Darcy.

Meanwhile, Miss Hind had climbed out of the

hole. The PE teacher was in her dressing gown

and flip flops, and had lots of leaves and twigs

sticking out of her hair.

'Have a nice trip, Miss Hind?' said Mr Spooky.

'I don't know what happened there,' said Miss

Hind, dusting off her dressing gown. 'I was just

on my way to do some midnight forest bathing

when I fell into this large hole.'

Mr Spooky picked a few leaves out of Miss

Hind's hair. 'Well, it's a full moon. Strange

things happen.'

'What are you doing out here at night?' Miss Hind asked.

Mr Spooky coughed. 'Oh, you know, just checking the Pumpkin Patch,' he said.

Miss Hind nodded. 'Ah, of course. Well, good luck!' She waved and jogged off back towards the school.

Mr Spooky headed into the Pumpkin Patch. In the bushes, the children and the unicorns breathed a sigh of relief. At least he hadn't turned into a werewolf and eaten Miss Hind.

'I think we should go back to the school too,' said Raheem. Next to him Brave snorted and nodded.

Jake and Pegasus agreed with Raheem.

Even Darcy said she wanted to go back because she and Star were cold and bored.

Mira sighed. She'd really wanted to solve the mystery. She was still *sure* that something spooky was going on with Mr Spooky.

'Come on Dave,' she said, as the others started walking back down the path. 'I guess we can work out the mystery in the morning.'

There was no reply. Where was Dave?

Just then, Mira heard strange chomping and slurping noises coming from behind them.

'Wait!' Mira called after the others. 'Dave's still in the Pumpkin Patch.'

She turned back towards the Pumpkin Patch — just as a round orange shape rose out of the mist.

'Wh–wh–what's that?' said Jake, his voice shaking.

The round orange shape started moving towards them. Star squealed and hid behind Darcy, who peered into the darkness. 'It looks like a . . .'

'A were-pumpkin?' said Raheem anxiously.

Mira could see it more clearly now. Its huge pumpkin head swayed from side to side as it walked. Instead of hands and feet, it had hooves – and a plump, white little belly that looked very familiar . . .

Strange chomping and slurping noises came from the pumpkin.

'It's Dave!' cried Mira.

'Mr Spooky!' cried Jake, pointing at the pumpkin.

'Jake, we literally just said it's Dave,' said Darcy.

'NO!' said Jake.

Mira realised that Jake wasn't pointing at the

pumpkin. He was pointing behind it.

A shadow fell over the walking pumpkin as Mr Spooky loomed into view. Dave froze. The moonlight bounced off Dave's pumpkin head, and all the children held their breath.

Mr Spooky looked down.

'Aha, my plan is complete!' he said.

Then Mr Spooky bent down and picked up the pumpkin. Dave's legs wriggled in the air. The teacher turned and started to run back towards the school.

'BRING BACK DAVE!' cried Mira.

'What do we do?!' cried Jake.

'Stop him before he gets away!' yelled Darcy.

'He's too fast!' cried Raheem.

The children and the unicorns ran after Mr Spooky as fast as they could. But even with a pumpkin-trapped Dave in his arms, Mr Spooky could still run a lot faster than the children!

'He's going into the Teachers' Turret,' said

Mira. 'Why is he taking Dave in there? We have to follow him!'

'STOP!' shouted Raheem, his eyes looking a bit wild. 'We're not allowed up this late. We're definitely not allowed out of the dorms at night. But we're really, REALLY not allowed in the Teachers' Turret. That's school rule number seventy-nine!'

Darcy crossed her arms. 'Yeah, well, school rule number one hundred million and sixty-two is: don't let Dave get eaten by Mr Spooky! We're going in.'

The children and their unicorns went inside, with Raheem and Brave at the back of the group. The door creaked behind them.

Mira walked forwards through the darkness. She took a doughnut out of her bag, hoping Dave might smell it and find them. (He had a super-powered sense of smell when it came to snacks.)

Soon they were climbing a twisty, turny turret stone staircase. Even if they turned the lights on, it would be hard to see each other. The stairs twisted and turned so much that they made Mira feel a bit dizzy.

'Darcy, are you okay riding Star up these stairs?' Raheem asked.

There was no reply. In the gloom of the staircase, no one could see Darcy.

'Darcy? Where are you?' Jake called.

'Did . . . do you think . . . Mr Spooky . . .' said Raheem.

'Did Mr Spooky EAT DARCY?' shrieked Mira.

PING!

'What was that?' Jake cuddled up to Pegasus in fright.

'Oh, hey guys.'

At the sound of Darcy's voice,

the friends whirled around. Darcy and Star were

just coming out of the turret

lift and were checking

their reflections in

the lift mirror.

'We thought

Mr Spooky had

eaten you!' hissed

Jake.

'Why would he eat

me?' asked Darcy with a frown. 'He's a Zombie

Ghost Princess. Zombie Ghost Princesses don't

eat people.'

'What do they do then?' said Jake.

'They magic them into ghosts for their deadly

ghost army,' said Darcy. 'Everyone knows that.'

Mira looked down at the doughnut with a feeling of determination. She would NOT let Dave become a deadly ghost!

At that moment the shadowy corridor echoed with a thundering sound.

Was that footsteps . . . or hoofsteps?

CHAPTER EIGHT
Mr Spooky's Surprise

'Aaaarghhh!' yelled the children.

'Aaaarghhh!' yelled Mr Spooky.

The panicked unicorns scattered to the walls of the turret, shrieking loudly.

Mr Spooky put his hands up to his ears. They could see he was holding something.

'WATCH OUT!' Raheem peered at Mr Spooky through the darkness. 'He's got a . . . spoon?'

Mira looked too. Sure enough, Mr Spooky was holding a small spoon, though Mira could

see that the edge was covered in tiny spikes.

'IT'S WHAT HE USES TO EAT PEOPLE!' yelled Jake.

'Aaaarghhh!' the children screamed again.

'WHY ARE YOU ALL SCREAMING?' yelled Mr Spooky.

'WHY DID YOU EAT MADAME SHETLAND?' Jake yelled back.

'. . . WHAT?!' yelled Mr Spooky.

'And all the other teachers!' said Raheem.

'AND WHY DID YOU TRY TO EAT DAVE?' yelled Mira, pushing her way to the front of the group. She wasn't scared of Mr Spooky OR his small, spiky spoon. Nothing would stop her standing up for her UBFF.

Mr Spooky blinked and stared at her. He was looking extremely confused.

There was a surprised-sounding burp from behind Mira. She turned round to see Dave. He *also* looked extremely confused. He pointed at Mr Spooky and shook his head.

Mira stared at her unicorn. 'Dave, are you trying to tell me that Mr Spooky DIDN'T try to eat you?'

Dave nodded, and did another spooky poo.

Mr Spooky burst out laughing. 'Why would I try to eat *Dave*?' he said.

'Because you're a vampire!' said Jake at the same time as Raheem said, 'Because you're a werewolf!'

'You kidnapped Dave when he was trapped in the pumpkin. We saw you,' said Mira. 'And then you ran off and brought him back here, to your lair. But Dave escaped because he's so clever.'

Dave burped.

Mr Spooky laughed again. 'Oh, no! I didn't realise Dave was IN the pumpkin. I was absolutely dazzled by the perfect pumpkin, and I couldn't wait to get it back here. As soon as I realised I'd accidentally picked up a unicorn as well, I popped the pumpkin off his head and here he is.'

Dave certainly didn't look like anyone had tried to eat him. It seemed like Mr Spooky was telling the truth.

'I'm sorry to have caused you a panic,' said Mr Spooky. 'And even though you shouldn't technically be sneaking out –' he raised an eyebrow – 'it was very brave of you to come looking for Dave. That's the true spirit of Unicorn School.'

Mira felt a warm glow in her chest. She grinned at Dave and gave him a scratch behind the ears. Dave did a happy fart.

'Excuse me, can we rewind?' said Darcy, putting her hand up. 'You were dazzled by the perfect pumpkin?'

Mr Spooky smiled a big-toothed smile at them. 'Well, I didn't want to ruin the spooky surprise, but since you're up here . . .'

Mr Spooky unlocked Madame Shetland's office. As he opened the door, Mira could see a glowing light coming from within the room. Everyone followed him inside. Raheem hovered at the door until Darcy dragged him in too.

The walls of the office were covered in strange shadows. And they saw where the glow was coming from.

Before them was an enormous table full of intricately carved pumpkins, with lights flickering inside them.

'Wow,' Mira gasped. 'They're beautiful.'

They really were. Each pumpkin had a
different scene carved into it. One showed
hundreds of tiny unicorns in a meadow. A
little cluster of pumpkins had been carved
to look like the Fearsome Forest, and on an
absolutely enormous pumpkin right in the
middle was a carving of Unicorn School itself.

Twinkling fairy lights were woven through the pumpkins, giving a magical sparkly glow to the scene.

Mr Spooky blushed. 'I'm so pleased you like them. I've been working really hard on them.'

For a few moments the children and the unicorns stood in silence, looking at the lovely display. Then Darcy got bored and started trying to nose around Madame Shetland's office and Raheem told her to stop.

Mr Spooky picked something up from the floor. It was the giant pumpkin that Dave had got stuck in.

'I'm so pleased Dave helped me find this,' said Mr Spooky. 'It's just perfect for adding the final

108

touch to my spooky surprise display.'

He put the pumpkin on the table and then raised his spiky spoon. Mira realised it must be a special spoon for carving pumpkins.

Just then Dave scuttled forwards and took a big bite out of the pumpkin. Then he scuttled back behind Mira.

'Dave!' said Darcy.

'You've ruined Mr Spooky's perfect pumpkin!' said Jake. Pegasus snorted crossly.

Mira stared at Mr Spooky. He was looking closely at the chomp mark in the pumpkin.

'This is brilliant!' he said.

The children and the unicorns all looked at each other. What did he mean?

'Look,' said Mr Spooky, pointing at the bite mark.

And then Mira realised what Mr Spooky meant. The bitemark was in the exact shape of a ghost!

'Well done, Dave!' said Mira, grinning at her unicorn.

'Do you want to help me carve the rest of the pumpkin, Dave?' said Mr Spooky.

Dave nodded and did a happy trot back over to the table.

'What shall we carve next?' said Mr Spooky.

'A vampire,' said Jake.

'A werewolf?' said Raheem.

'A Zombie Ghost Princess!' said Darcy.

'Let's do them ALL!' said Mr Spooky.

The children cheered, the unicorns clapped their hooves and Dave started chomp-carving the pumpkin. The others took turns using the spiky spoon to scoop out the pumpkin insides, which Dave also ate. Mr Spooky popped some fairy lights inside.

'Spooky surprise complete!' he said, looking pleased.

Mira looked at the glowing pumpkin display.
It was totally awesome. Then she looked at
the flickering shadows on the wall of Madame
Shetland's office, which made her think . . .

'Mr Spooky, where *is* Madame Shetland?'
she asked him.

Mr Spooky turned to them, his face suddenly
serious.

'Ah, now you mustn't breathe a word,' he said,
'but Madame Shetland is a zombie ghost.'

CHAPTER NINE
Zombie Ghost Princess

There was silence.

'I TOLD you!' said Darcy, looking round at everyone.

'Wh-wh-what about the other teachers?' said Jake. Behind him, Pegasus shivered.

'They're zombie ghosts too,' said Mr Spooky. 'Shall we go and say hi?'

'Is that safe?' asked Raheem. Brave snorted.

But Mr Spooky was already walking past them, out of Madame Shetland's office. He walked up the steps to the room at the very top of the Teachers' Turret: the staff room.

The children and unicorns followed. Mira couldn't wait to tell her sister that she'd actually seen inside the staff room – as long as zombie ghosts didn't eat her before she got the chance.

They walked through the door into a large, octagonal room with windows open to the sky outside. Mira saw wispy clouds crossing over the moon. Clusters of candles in the corners of the room gave everything a dusting of dim lighting.

'Yoo hoo!' said Mr Spooky.

Mira held her breath. She'd never seen a zombie before. Or a ghost. And definitely not a zombie ghost. Next to her, Dave did a tiny, frightened fart.

'WOOOOOOOOOOOEEUUURRRRRRGGGGGH!'

The ghostly groaning sound was coming from a corner of the staff room, where there was a sofa and some chairs.

Jake pointed at the sofa. 'L-l-look!' he said.

They all looked to where he was pointing.

A greyish, greenish hand was gripping the edge of the sofa. On the other side of the sofa another hand appeared, then another one wrapped around one of the chairs.

'Arghhhhhhh!' screeched the children and the unicorns.

Then a head popped up from behind the chair. Mira could see it was Ms Dazzleflank, but her hair was covered in cobwebs.

'**WOOOOOEEEEEURRRGGGH!**' she groaned.

'I can't believe it,' whispered Darcy. 'It's even worse than a Zombie Ghost Princess. It's a ZOMBIE GHOST TEACHER.'

Another head popped up from behind another chair. It was Zombie Ghost Mr Nosebag. Other teachers popped up and lurched forwards, all with grey-green skin and covered in cobwebs, groaning in a ghostly way.

Then cushions flew out from the sofa, to reveal Zombie Ghost Miss Glitterhorn lying across it. She groaned again.

The children and unicorns stared with open mouths. They couldn't believe what they were seeing!

'Um, I think maybe we should RUN?' said Raheem.

Even Darcy nodded. They turned back towards the door. But as they did, a loud drum beat started up.

The children and unicorns stopped running. Star skidded into a wall.

'Don't go yet. They've only just started!' called Mr Spooky.

Mira and the others turned back towards the Zombie Ghost Teachers. The Zombie Ghost Teachers had started jerking their limbs in time to the music. An electronic guitar kicked in and they started doing a series of complicated leaps and jumps and lunges.

Miss Glitterhorn joined in from the sofa.

'What is happening?' said Darcy, her eyes wide.

'Should we still run?' said Raheem.

Mira wasn't sure. It wasn't clear if the Zombie

Ghost Teachers were going to eat them or just
dance at them.

PHWWEEEET!

Her thoughts were interrupted by the familiar
sound of Miss Hind's PE whistle. The music cut

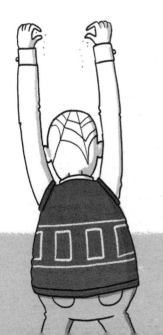

out, and the PE teacher came marching over from the other side of the staff room. Zombie Ghost Ms Dazzleflank bent double, catching her breath, and Zombie Ghost Mr Nosebag sat down on a chair.

'That was RUBBISH!' yelled Miss Hind. 'Do it again.'

'Can we have a little rest?' said Mr Nosebag with a wheeze.

'NO,' said Miss Hind.

'I thought it was great!' said Mr Spooky, and gave them a round of applause.

Star started to clap her hooves together too, but when she saw no one else was clapping she stopped.

The Zombie Ghost Teachers – who Mira
could see now were actually just their normal
teachers wearing ghostly make-up and costumes
– turned to look at them. Darcy waved.

'What are they doing up here?' thundered
Miss Hind. 'No children allowed in the
Teachers' Turret. That's school rule number
seventy-eight.'

'Actually, it's school rule number seventy-ni—'

'We were just helping Mr Spooky with his
pumpkins!' said Mira, interrupting Raheem.

'Ah yes, these guys were just helping me out
with my spooky surprise,' said Mr Spooky. 'I'm
sure they will keep your spooky surprise a secret
too!'

'Hmmm.' Miss Hind narrowed her eyes.

'Can we get on with it, please?' came a voice from above them. Mira looked up to see Madame Shetland suspended from the ceiling in a harness. She had the grey-green facepaint and cobwebs too, but was also wearing a crown.

'*Madame Shetland* is the Zombie Ghost Princess!' said Darcy.

'Yes, Darcy,' the head teacher called down as she swung violently from side to side in her harness. 'But as Mr Spooky says, you mustn't spoil the surprise for the rest of the school.'

'So is this why all the teachers have been disappearing?' Mira said.

'Yes. Miss Hind has got us on a very intensive training regime, with extra sessions for some of us, which has meant Mr Spooky has had to cover *lots* of our lessons,' said Ms Dazzleflank, wiping the sweat off her face. 'And Miss Glitterhorn pulled all the muscles in her leg in the first rehearsal.'

Miss Glitterhorn gave them a wave from the sofa. She actually looked quite comfortable.

Mira could see she had a book tucked behind one of the cushions.

'Enough chit-chat,' said Miss Hind. 'Back to it!'

'Children, you all need to go to bed,' said Miss Glitterhorn. 'It's kind of you to help Mr Spooky, but you need to be feeling fresh for your own spooky surprise at the party tomorrow. I can't wait to see what you've come up with!'

Mira's eyes went wide. They'd been so busy worrying about whether Mr Spooky was a vampire or a zombie or a werewolf, they hadn't prepared anything at all!

'Yes,' said Mira quickly. 'We have to go and, um, finish our spooky surprise right now,

which we have definitely planned!'

Ms Dazzleflank clapped her hands. 'Oh, wonderful, children! I do hope you have very dramatic plans.'

'Absolutely, Ms Dazzleflank. Come on, team, let's go back to the dorms!' Mira ushered her friends out of the spooky turret and into the lift.

'We absolutely do not have a plan though,' said Jake.

Mira took out her notebook.

'See,' said Jake, pointing to where Mira had written *Really Good Spooky Surprise Ideas* at the top of a totally empty page. 'We have zero ideas on there.'

Mira sighed, looking down at the empty page.

Jake was right. But then her eyes flicked over to the other page.

'Don't worry Jake,' said Mira. 'I know JUST what we can do!'

CHAPTER TEN
Spoooooooky Celebrations

The very next day it was time for the big Unicorn School Halloween Party! There had been fun stuff going on all day and now the sun was setting. The Grand Hall was draped in sparkly cobwebs and there were unicorn-skull-shaped piñatas everywhere (Dave loved knocking those down to get the treats inside), as well as toffee apples to bob for, trick-or-treat tins and lots and lots of sweets and other spooky party food.

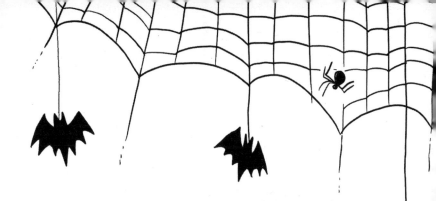

Mr Spooky's pumpkin display glowed in
the corner of the hall, and everyone spent ages
looking at all the cool details he'd carved on
the pumpkins. Dave's ghostly bite-carving was
particularly impressive.

Ms Dazzleflank was DJ-ing and the
dancefloor was packed. Mr Spooky led
everybody in the Monster Macarena and even
Miss Hind took her unicorn, Simon, for a spin.

Mira and her friends were glad that Mr
Spooky wasn't a vampire or a werewolf after all.
They were only a little bit disappointed that he

wasn't a Zombie Ghost Princess.

Earlier that day, Class Yellow had hidden under the tables at breakfast and jumped out at everybody on their way into the dining hall. As spooky surprises go, it was a bit of a rubbish effort, but Dave liked it because he could pretend to be scared and run straight to the front of the food queue.

Rani, Lois and and her friends had spent all day dressed up as spooky statues that looked completely real until someone walked past and they creeeeaaaakkked into a different position. It was really cool.

Freya, Tamsin and Seb made the most enormous slime splurge that slopped down the grand staircase. It was a bit more gross than spooky, but because it was green and sparkly no one minded.

So far the biggest surprise had been when Dave levitated by the spooky snack table, but Mira had to explain that this wasn't their spooky surprise – it was just one of Dave's particularly powerful hover-farts.

Mira checked her watch and then grinned at Dave. It was finally time to head back to the dorm. They'd been waiting until it was dark to share their spooky surprise with everyone!

'Come on, Dave!' she said to her unicorn, who had his head in the Halloween bucket again. In the end she dragged him with her, while he dragged the bucket, and they headed off towards the dorm.

THE DANGERS OF HALLOWEEN

Mira peeped through a crack in the curtain as pupils, teachers and unicorns filed into the

dorm. Her heart was thumping in her chest, mostly from excitement and a little bit from nerves. She really wanted the spooky surprise to go well! They hadn't had very much time to prepare, but they'd all worked together as a team and she was really proud of all her friends.

Mira was crouched on a bunk bed, with a curtain draped over it so no one could see her. Around the dorm, all the other beds had curtains draped over them too. Mira hoped Dave was ready in his hiding position!

Click!

The lights went out and the dorm was plunged into darkness.

A hushed 'Ooooooh!' went around the room.

133

Mira got her torch ready, cleared her throat and wafted her curtain. Then she poked her head out, with her torch beaming under her chin.

'It was a dark and spooky night,' Mira said. 'And the Forest of Death was FULL of spooky surprises.' She stepped out through the curtains. 'Follow me, if you DARE . . .' she said, and everyone shuffled round. 'Past the lonely mountain rock.' She stepped round a pile of coats, 'there is a creepy old castle, high on a hill.' Mira was standing in front of the next bunk bed now. 'And in that creepy old castle there are . . . VAMPIRES!'

The curtains on the bunk bed flew open, and Jake and Pegasus leaped out, wearing capes and plastic fangs and with jam smeared over their faces.

'MWA HA HA HA!!' roared Jake and Pegasus gave a terrifying whinny.

The crowd screamed.

'But that isn't the spookiest surprise on this dark and spooky night,' said Mira, stepping across to the bunk bed on the other side of the room. 'Come with me, further through the dark, dark forest to the petrifying Pumpkin Patch, where WEREWOLVES lurk!'

'Awoooooooo!' howled Raheem, as the curtain flew up to reveal him and Brave, wearing furry jumpers and fake claws. Around them were Mr Spooky's pumpkins with flickering fairy lights.

'Oooooh!' gasped the crowd, but then they screamed as Raheem and Brave leaped out towards them, howling and growling.

'Quick, run away!' called Mira, running to the next bunk bed, and the crowd shuffled after her.

'Oh no!' cried Mira, skidding to a stop by the bed. 'We have accidentally run into an EVEN SPOOKIER part of the Forest of Death. This is the Gloomy Graveyard. Nothing lives here.'

'Phew,' said a girl from Class Orange.

'Because Zombie Ghost Princesses are TOTALLY DEAD!' yelled Darcy, bursting through the curtains.

Darcy and Star were wearing zombie ghost outfits and were sitting on the bunk bed among gravestones made out of cereal boxes painted grey. Darcy improvised a musical called 'Zombie Ghost Princess' where she played all the characters. After fifteen minutes with no sign of it stopping, Mira quietly drew the curtains over them and went over to the window.

'But there is ONE MORE spooky surprise tonight,' she whispered dramatically.

A hush descended on the room.

'Because now we are in the furthest depths of the forest,' said Mira. 'And this is where you find the Spooky McSpookiest thing of all.'

'What could it be?' gasped Seb.

'Is it a massive witch??' stammered Tamsin.

'It has red eyes,' said Mira. 'And a bone-chilling neigh. It is the spookiest of all unicorns. That's right, it's the . . . **SPOOKICORN!**'

There was a flash of lightning. And on the

other side of the window, in the dark of the
night, there appeared a terrifying unicorn with
glowing red eyes. It threw back its head and gave
a bone-chilling neigh. Then it vanished.

Everyone screamed, even Mira!

Everyone burst into applause and Mira bowed
deeply.

After the clapping had died down and
everyone had left the room, Mira pushed
the window open and leaned out. 'You were
amazing as the Spookicorn, Dave! You can
come in now!'

But there was no sign of Dave.

'Er, Mira?' called Raheem.

Mira looked over. Seb was standing next

to Dave, who was curled up in a ball in the corner of the room, fast asleep. He was in his Spookicorn costume, with a glittery wig and red eyeshadow that Darcy had put on him.

'He's been here the whole time . . .' said Darcy.

They all looked back at the window.

But there was nothing there . . .

∪∪∪

'I'm sure we all imagined it,' said Darcy, as they hurried back towards the Great Hall.

'Yeah,' said Mira, but she wasn't so sure. Maybe the Spookicorn did exist, after all . . .

Back in the Grand Hall it was time for the teachers' zombie ghost dance. It was completely brilliant – even though some of the teachers

forgot the moves and Miss Hind lost her temper and threw a pumpkin at the wall (which Darcy said was her favourite bit).

Then it was time to award the Spooky Surprise medal. Mira's team huddled together.

'We've had some amazing spooky surprise efforts,' said Madame Shetland.

'But we could see how much effort had gone into the winning entry – especially when this person has been so busy. The winner is . . . the Perfect Pumpkin Patch, by Mr Spooky and Dave!'

Everyone clapped and cheered.

'Yay! Go Dave!' yelled Mira, jumping up and down and nudging her UBFF towards the stage.

Mr Spooky grinned from ear to ear as Madame Shetland handed him his medal. She hung Dave's medal round his neck.

'It's so lovely to win this,' said Mr Spooky. 'But I feel like we're ALL winners here . . .'

'It's ghost football all over again,' said Darcy.

'So I've made everyone a medal,' Mr Spooky continued. 'Out of pumpkin!'

Everyone cheered again as Mr Spooky threw the pumpkin medals into the crowd.

'And this is a lovely way to say goodbye,' said Mr Spooky. 'Now your teachers are back in action, I'm off on another fun adventure!'

Everyone cheered again and waved.

And Mr Spooky disappeared in a puff of smoke.

'Did you see that?' said Jake.

'I KNEW he was spooky!' said Mira.

Then there was a loud coughing from the side of the stage.

'Oh, he just went behind the smoke machine,' said Darcy. 'He's still there.'

'You know,' said Mira, 'there are so many

brilliant things about Unicorn School but the BEST thing is getting to hang out with you guys.'

'It definitely is,' said Raheem, and Brave wiped away a tear.

'A MILLION per cent,' said Darcy. 'Now let's get back to what we're best at. Being awesome!'

They found the rest of Class Red and everyone danced happily to the spooky music.

Mira and Dave did all the spooky dance moves: the Zombie, the Robot, the Evil Kitten and the Killer Worm. Mira thought again how lucky she was to have an amazing, unique UBFF like Dave.

Dave stopped spinning around and Mira gave

her unicorn a hoof-five followed by a huge hug.

Then Dave did the most enormous poo EVER

seen in Unicorn School.

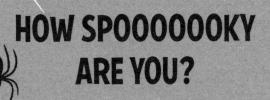

HOW SPOOOOOOKY ARE YOU?

Answer these creepy questions to find out just how scary YOU like to be on Halloween!

1. When trick-or-treaters ring your doorbell, what do you do?
   a. Open the door wearing your favourite scary costume then jump out to shout, 'BOO!'
   b. You're not there to open the door to trick or treaters! You're out and about scaring people...
   c. Ignore the door and eat all the treats yourself.
   d. Hide under the bed.

2. When you go trick-or-treating, what do you wear?
   a. You have LOTS of costumes! Maybe a witch's pointy hat and cloak . . . or a big sheet to be a spooky ghost . . . Or you wear fangs to be a spooky vampire!
   b. You don't need to dress up – you ALWAYS give off spooky vibes!
   c. It doesn't matter what you wear, it's ALL about the treats!
   d. Your special superhero cape.

3. What kind of face would you carve in a pumpkin for a lantern?
    a. A cute little kitticorn face with extra-long fangs.
    b. A truly terrifying scene featuring demons and ghostly ghouls.
    c. You'd eat your way into the pumpkin to make a truly unique image.
    d. A picture of your BFF.

4. How would you start a spooky story?
    a. It was a dark and stormy night . . .
    b. ALL the stories you tell are spooky . . .
    c. Once upon a time, in a land made of sweets and treats . . .
    d. Once upon a time there was a super brave unicorn . . .

Answers:

Mostly As: you love Halloween, just like Mira! You're just the right amount of spooky!

Mostly Bs: EEK! Are you the Spookicorn?!

Mostly Cs: You are just like Dave. You love spooky Halloween snacks and treats and are full of spooky fun!

Mostly Ds: You're like Raheem's unicorn. Brave! You find Halloween a BIT scary but you love hanging out with all of your friends.

Catch up on all of Mira and Dave's adventures at Unicorn School!

EGMONT

Look out for more AMAZING adventures with Mira and Dave – coming soon!